D

JE MA

Fluffy McWhiskers was cute.

Dangerously cute.

Yes, Fluffy McWhiskers was
so cute that if you saw her . . .

KA

you'd explode.

Elephants, snakes, platypuses, even a cute little koala.
If you saw Fluffy McWhiskers . . .

So cute!

This, of course, made Fluffy very sad and extremely lonely.

She tried to fix her problem.

An ugly sweater.

A bad haircut.

Well, here goes nothing!

But nothing worked.
They only made her cuter!

She even tried wearing
a paper bag over her head . . .

KABOOM!

but that was
ridiculously cute!

Just when she thought it couldn't get any worse . . .
they published her picture in the newspaper.

That's when things got out of hand . . .

KABOOM!

Fluffy McWhiskers had no choice:
she needed to go somewhere
far, far away, where no one
would find her.

Eventually she found exactly what she was looking for.

Fluffy tried again.

The island was perfect.

True, volleyball was not so much fun.

Getting her tummy scratched required a lot of work.

And pizza took forever to be delivered.

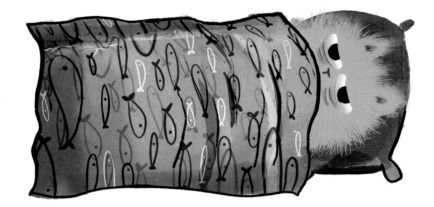

But Fluffy could eat, sleep, read,
and even watch the stars from her super cute telescope,
day
after day,
night
after night. . . .

Again she tried to fix the problem, but . . .

BurP!

she got hungry.

There Fluffy sat, day after day, night after night, getting cuter and cuter and fluffier and fluffier. Sometimes she tossed a letter out to sea to pass the time.

Until one day Fluffy heard a very unusual sound . . .

Fluffy freaked. Someone was on the island; someone had found her; someone was about to EXPLODE!

Fluffy tried to run, but there was nowhere to go, nowhere to hide.

PIZZA SLOTH EXPRESS

PIZZA SLOTH EXPRESS

So she closed her eyes and waited. . . .

Huh. Nothing!

"I don't understand," said Fluffy.
"Why didn't you explode . . . *DOG*?"

"I was going to ask you the same question . . . *CAT*,"
replied the extremely cute dog.

Volleyball suddenly became pretty awesome.

Getting her tummy scratched
required a lot less work.

Fluffy had finally found a friend!

Awwwww, how cute is that?